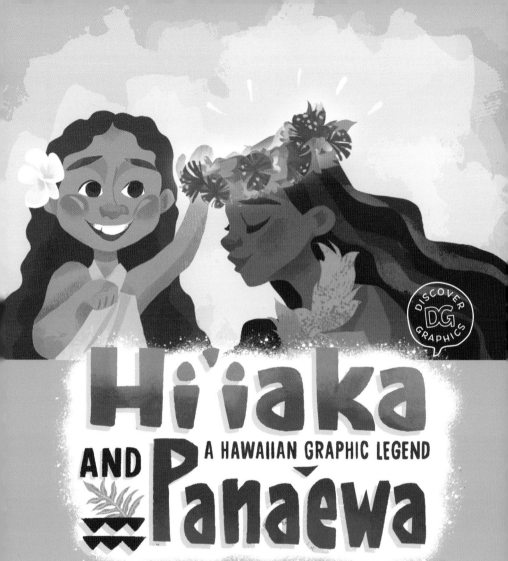

Hi'iaka

AND Panāēwa

A HAWAIIAN GRAPHIC LEGEND

BY GABRIELLE AHULI'I

ILLUSTRATED BY SARAH DEMONTEVERDE

PICTURE WINDOW BOOKS
a capstone imprint

Published by Picture Window Books, an imprint of Capstone
1710 Roe Crest Drive, North Mankato, Minnesota 56003
capstonepub.com

Library of Congress Cataloging-in-Publication Data is available on the Library of Congress website.

ISBN: 9781484672907 (hardcover)
ISBN: 9781484672853 (paperback)
ISBN: 9781484672860 (ebook PDF)

Summary: Hiʻiaka wants to make the forests of Hawaiʻi safe for people. But she'll have to battle an evil lizard named Panaʻewa and his army to do it. With a little help from her sister, her friend, and some special powers, she's ready for a great battle.

Editorial Credits
Editor: Ericka Smith; Designer: Kay Fraser;
Production Specialist: Katy LaVigne

Author's Note

Pasifika legends are an unbroken chain of narratives stretching back thousands of years. To honor that, I would like to *mahalo* (thank) the following sources for lending me their knowledge for this adaptation: *Hawaiʻi Island Legends* by Caroline Curtis and Mary Kawena Pukuʻi, *The Epic Tale of Hiʻiakaikapoliopele* by Hoʻoulumahiehie, and *ʻŌlelo Noʻeau* by Mary Kawena Pukuʻi. I hope our ancestors look on my telling with pride.

Printed and bound in the USA. 5195

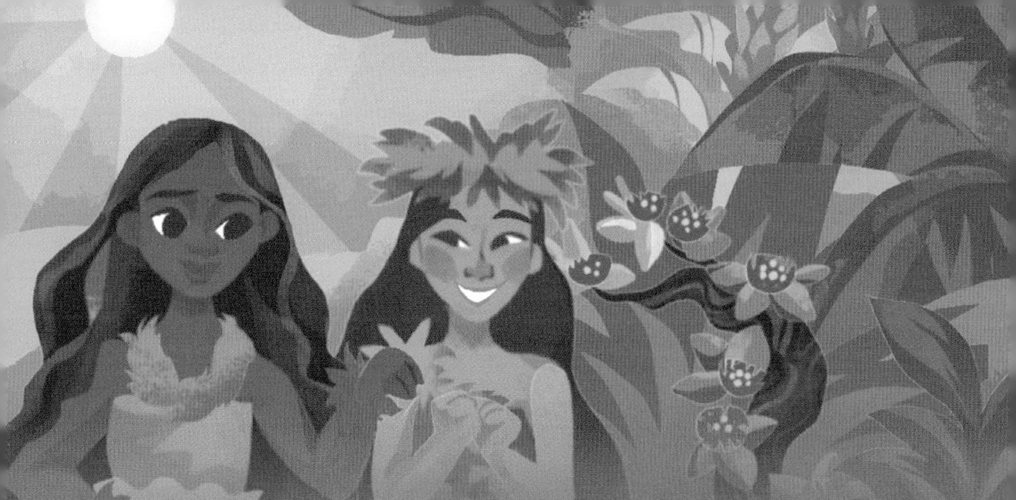

CAST OF CHARACTERS

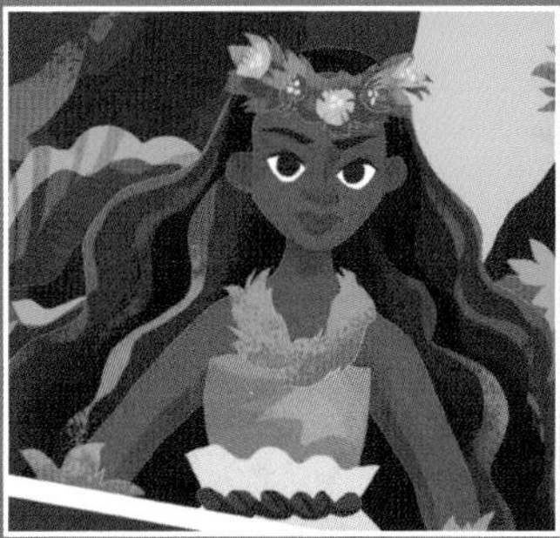

Hi‘iaka (HEE-ee-ah-kuh) is brave and wants to protect the island from Pana‘ewa.

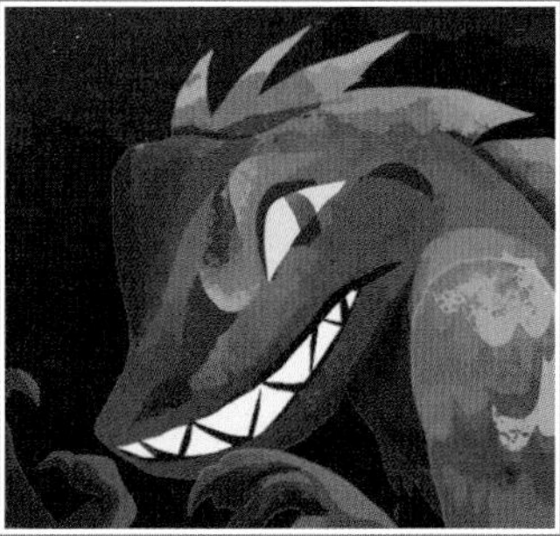

Pana‘ewa (Pah-NUH-ev-uh) is evil and wants to keep people and gods off the island.

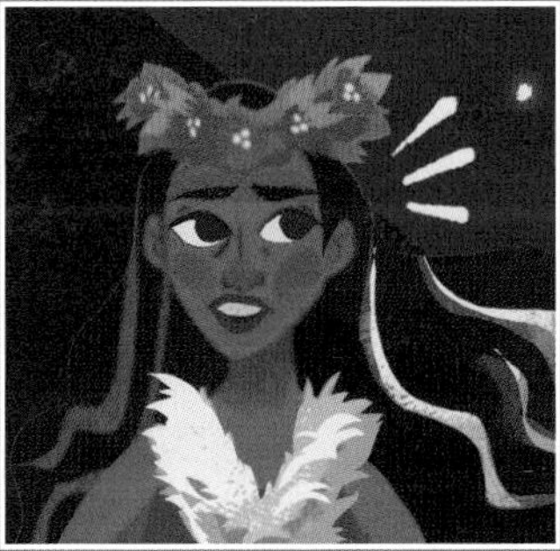

Pele (PEH-leh) loves her sister Hi‘iaka. She helps her try to protect the island.

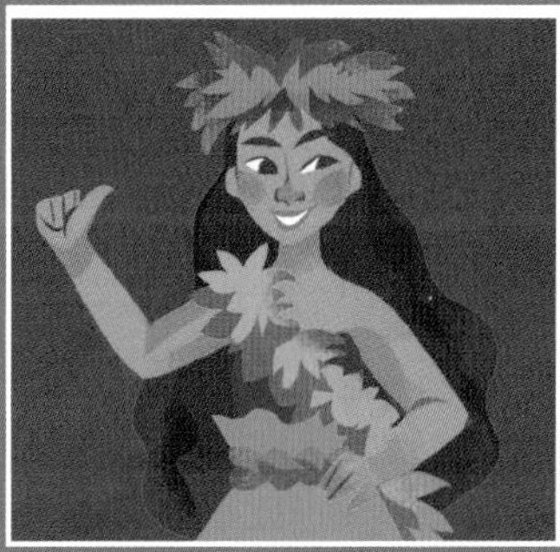

Wahine‘ōma‘o (Wah-HE-neh-oh-mah-oh) wants to help her friend Hi‘iaka. She is brave too.

HOW TO READ A GRAPHIC NOVEL

Graphic novels are easy to read. Boxes called panels show you how to follow the story. Look at the panels from left to right and top to bottom.

Read the word boxes and word balloons from left to right as well. Don't forget the sound and action words in the pictures.

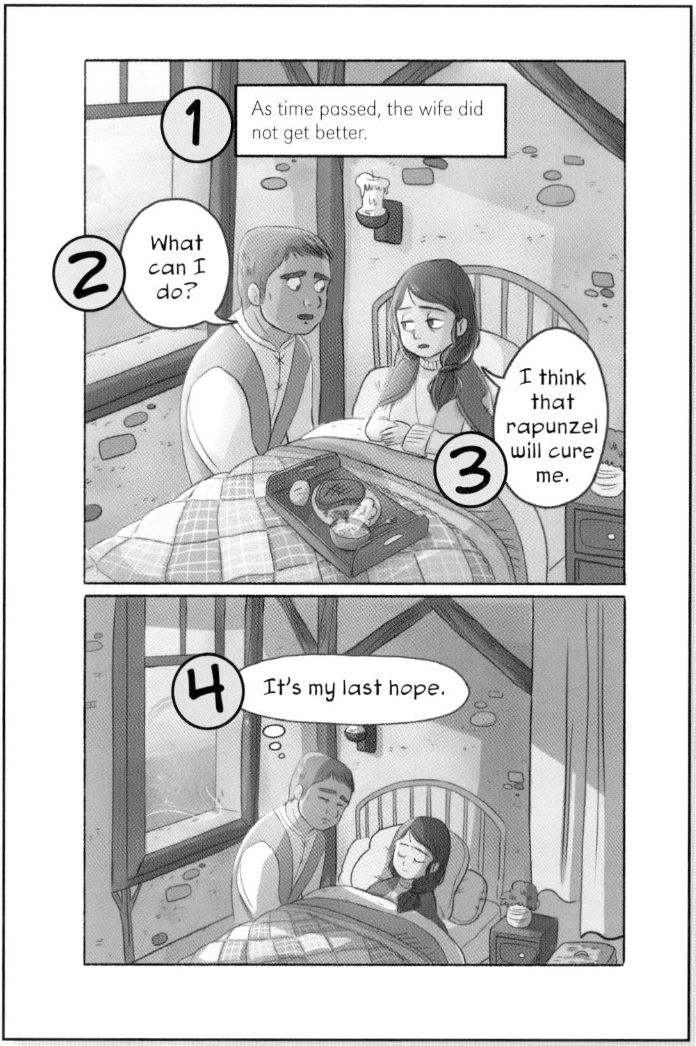
1
As time passed, the wife did not get better.
2
What can I do?
3
I think that rapunzel will cure me.
4
It's my last hope.

The pictures and the words work together to tell the whole story.

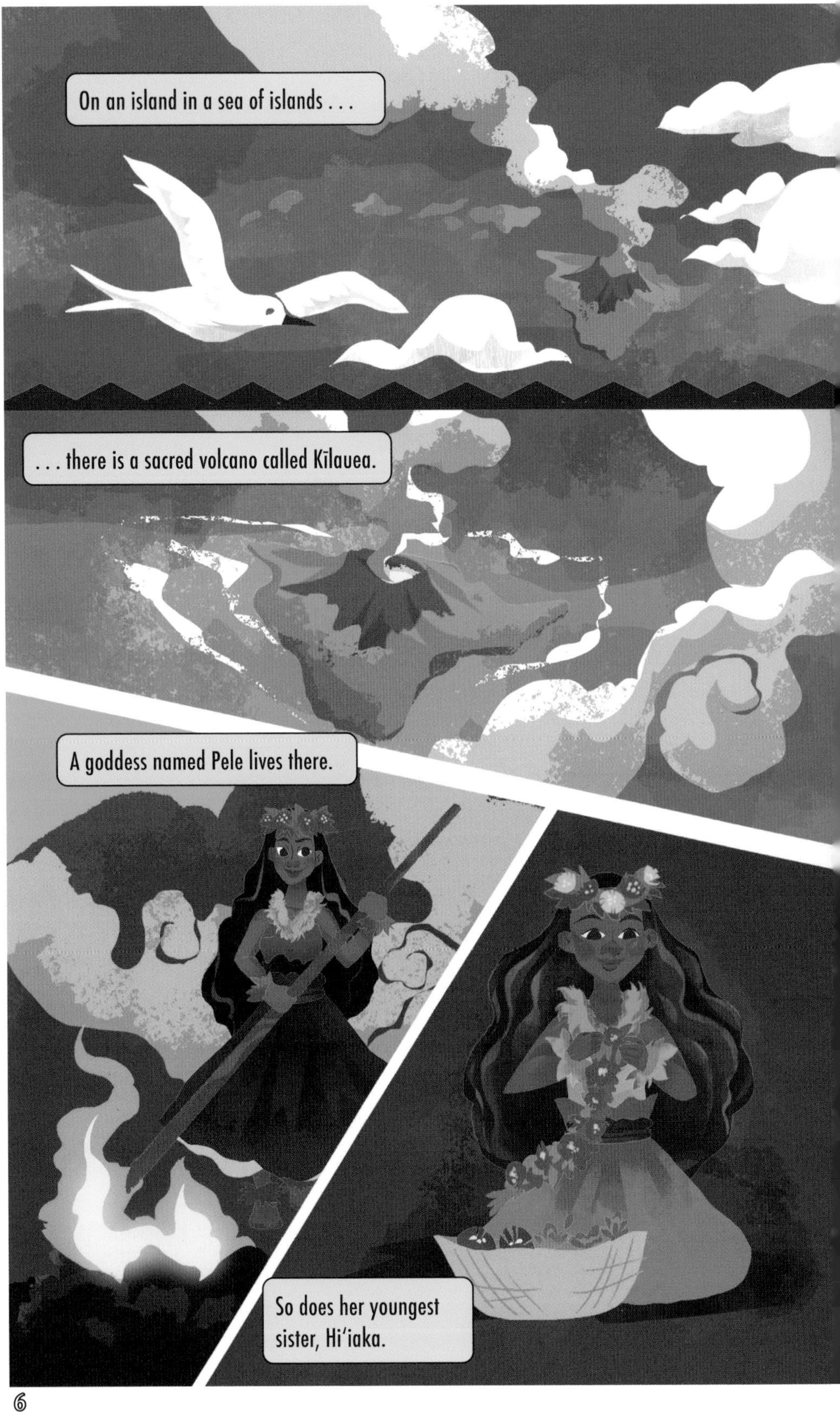
On an island in a sea of islands . . .
. . . there is a sacred volcano called Kīlauea.
A goddess named Pele lives there.
So does her youngest sister, Hi'iaka.

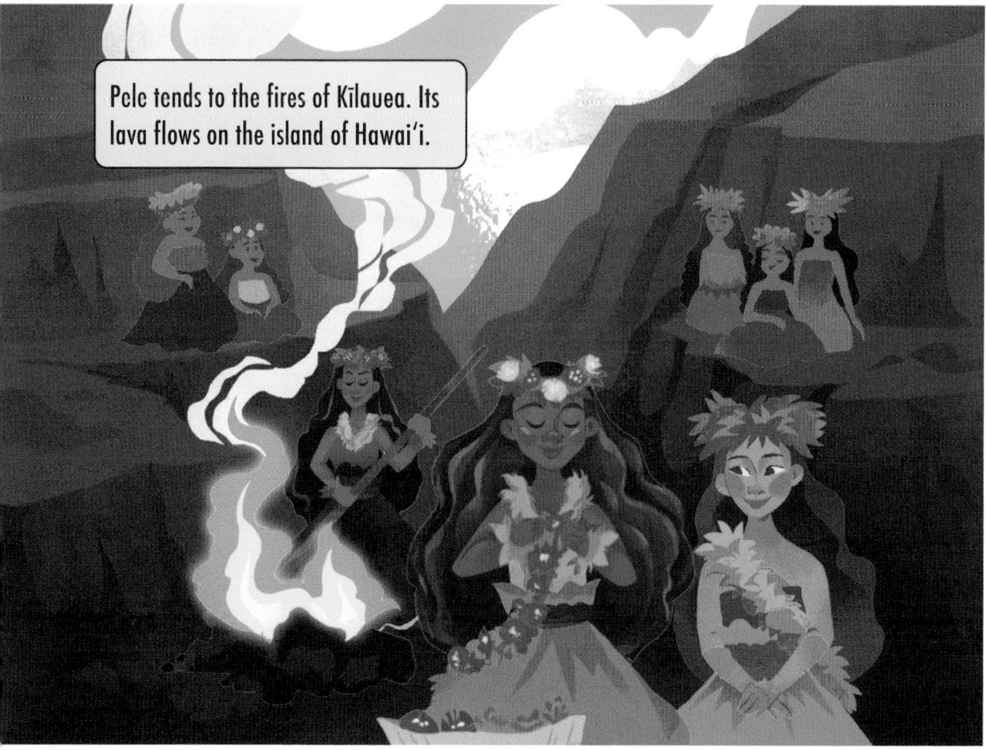
Pele tends to the fires of Kīlauea. Its lava flows on the island of Hawai'i.

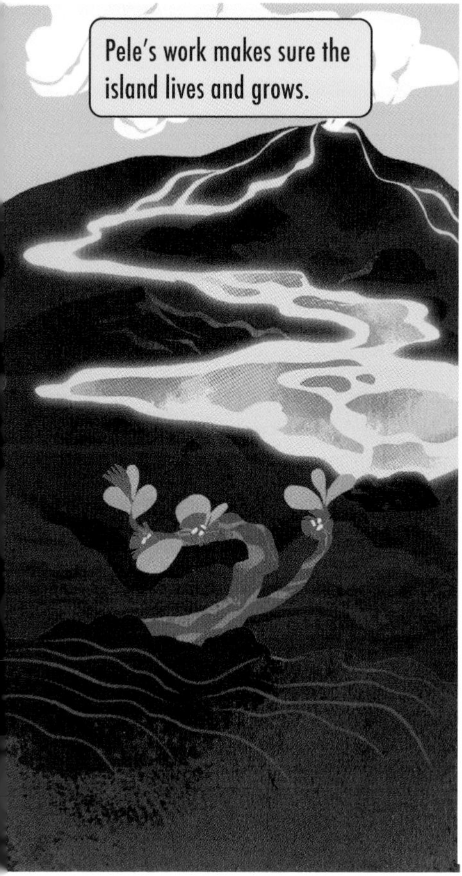
Pele's work makes sure the island lives and grows.

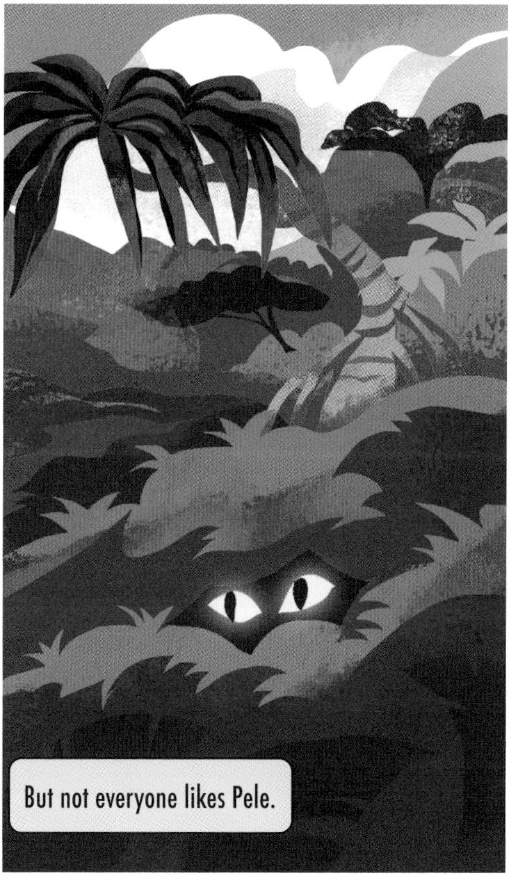
But not everyone likes Pele.

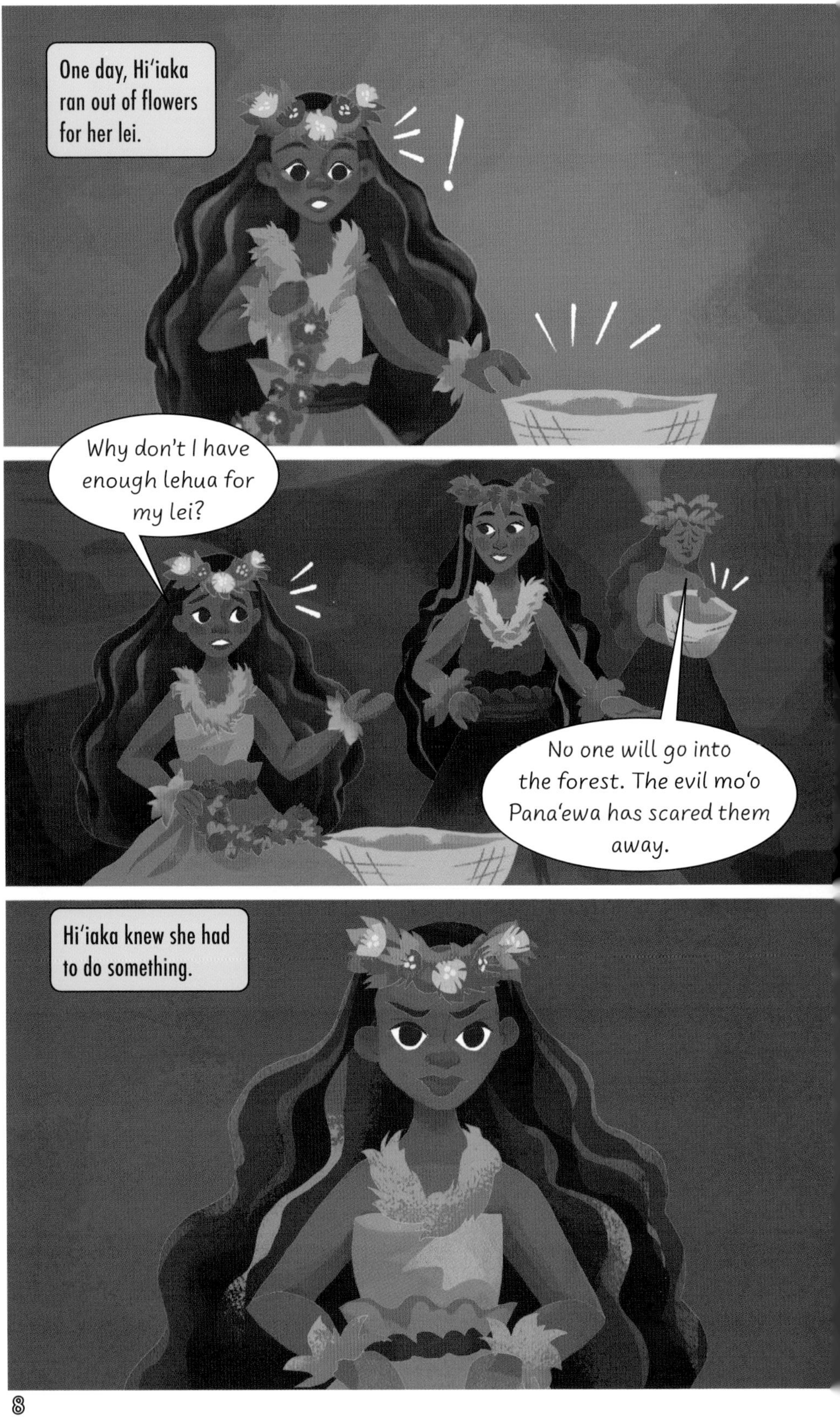
One day, Hi'iaka ran out of flowers for her lei.
Why don't I have enough lehua for my lei?
No one will go into the forest. The evil mo'o Pana'ewa has scared them away.
Hi'iaka knew she had to do something.

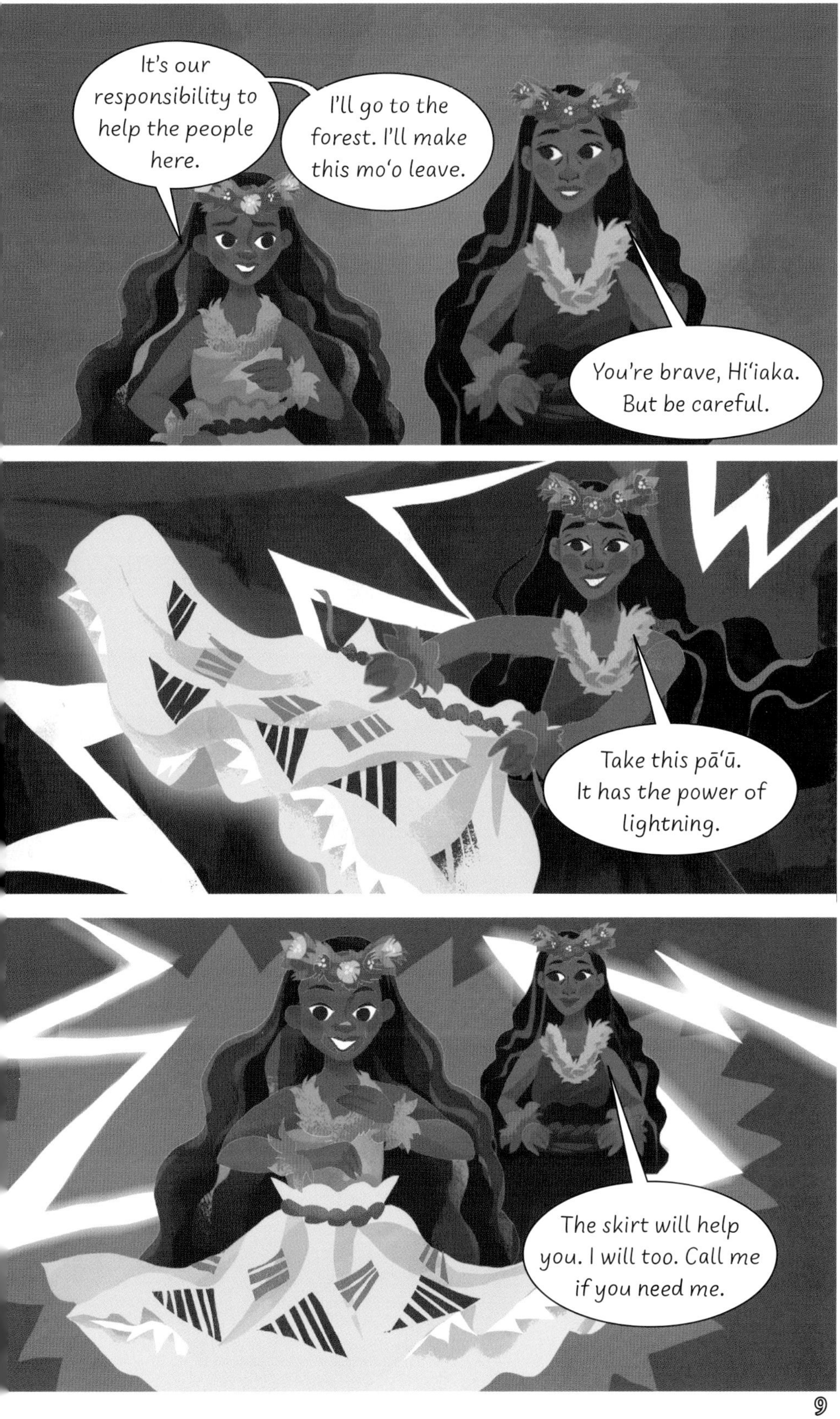
It's our responsibility to help the people here.
I'll go to the forest. I'll make this mo'o leave.
You're brave, Hi'iaka. But be careful.
Take this pā'ū. It has the power of lightning.
The skirt will help you. I will too. Call me if you need me.

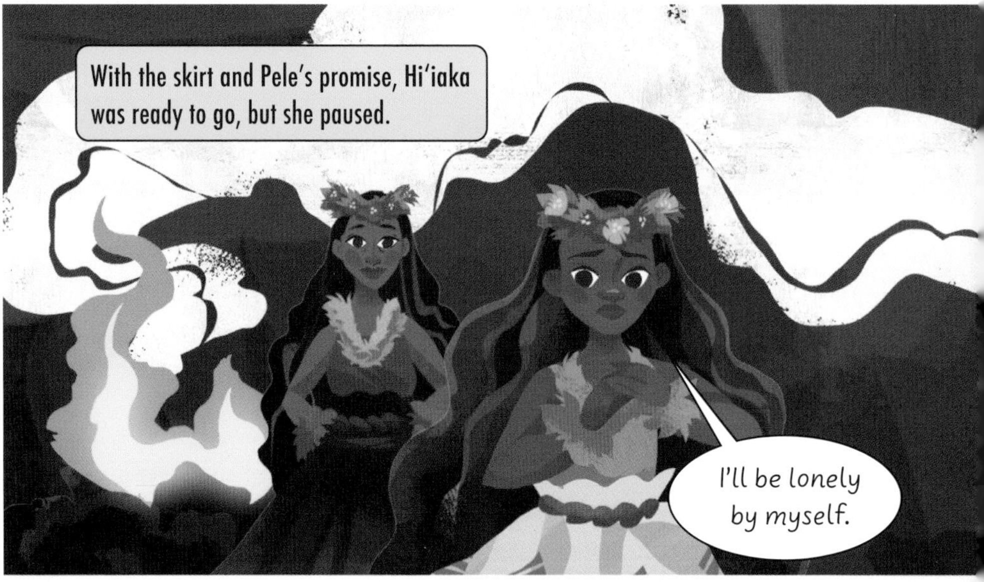
With the skirt and Pele's promise, Hi'iaka was ready to go, but she paused.
I'll be lonely by myself.

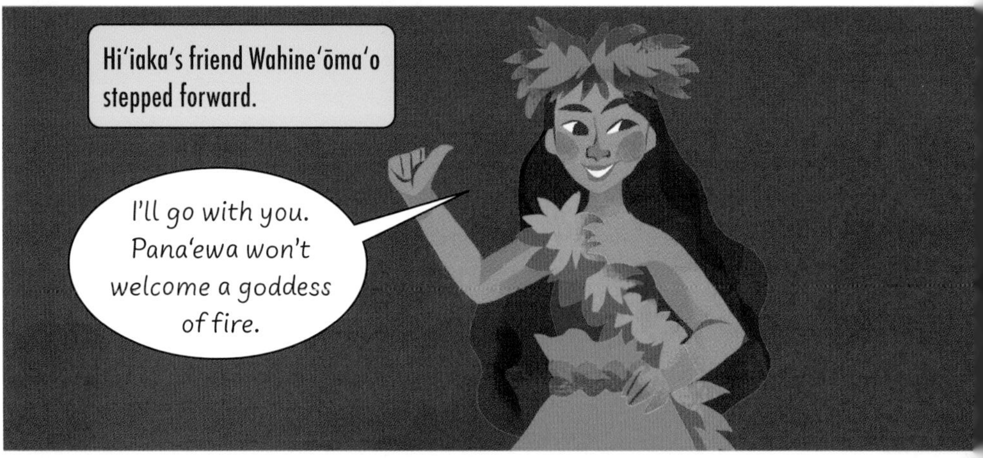
Hi'iaka's friend Wahine'ōma'o stepped forward.
I'll go with you. Pana'ewa won't welcome a goddess of fire.

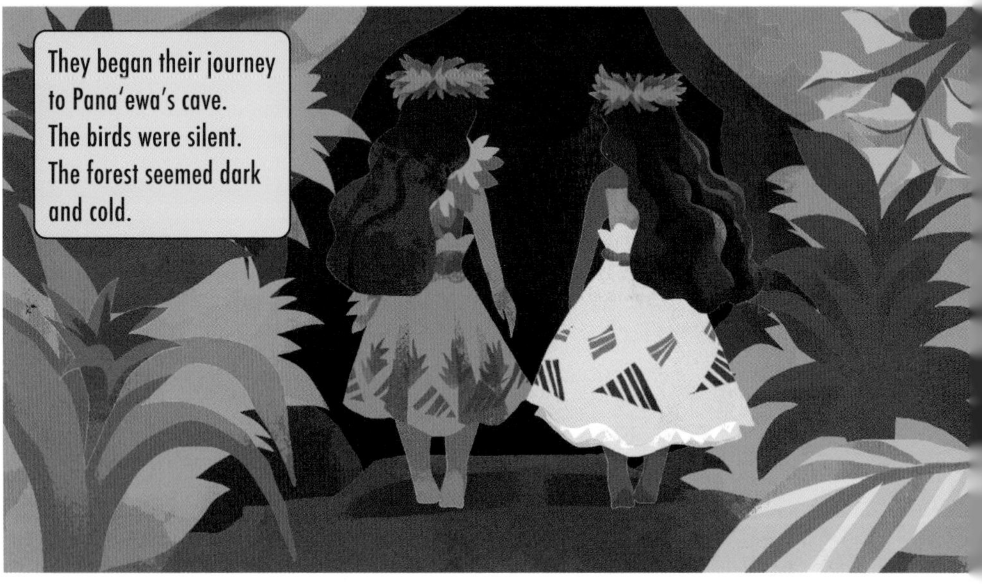
They began their journey to Pana'ewa's cave. The birds were silent. The forest seemed dark and cold.

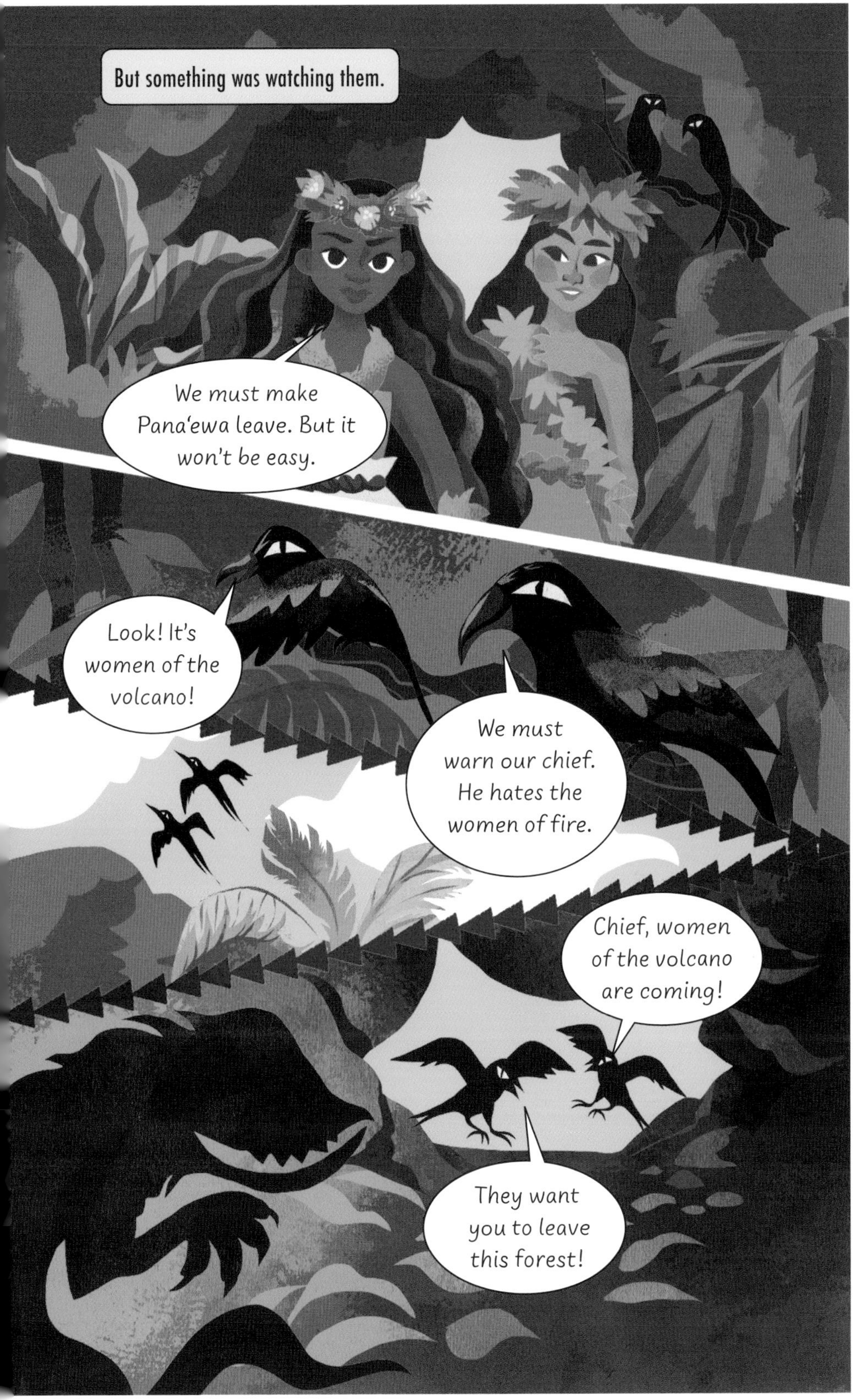
But something was watching them.
We must make Pana'ewa leave. But it won't be easy.
Look! It's women of the volcano!
We must warn our chief. He hates the women of fire.
Chief, women of the volcano are coming!
They want you to leave this forest!

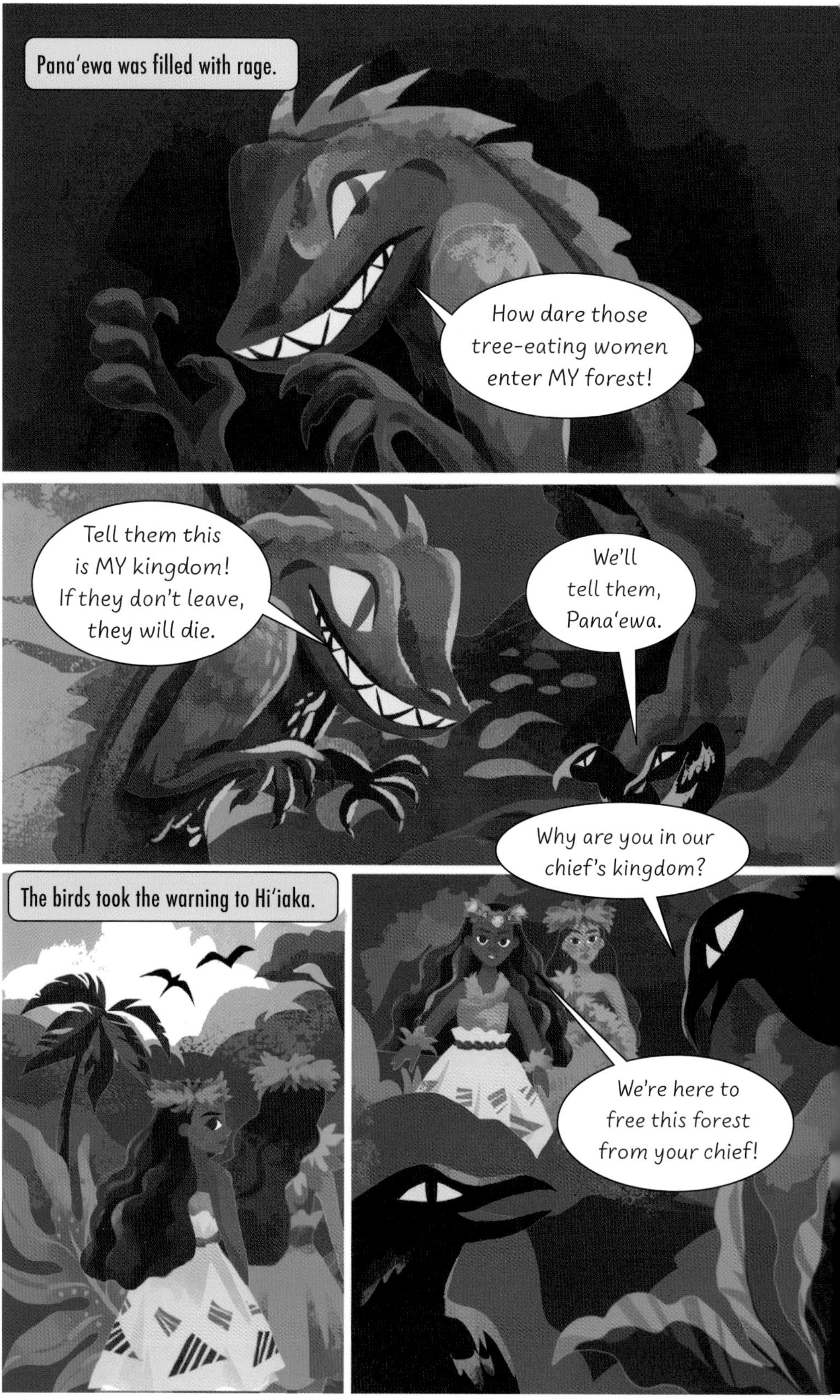
Pana‘ewa was filled with rage.
How dare those tree-eating women enter MY forest!
Tell them this is MY kingdom! If they don't leave, they will die.
We'll tell them, Pana‘ewa.
The birds took the warning to Hi‘iaka.
Why are you in our chief's kingdom?
We're here to free this forest from your chief!

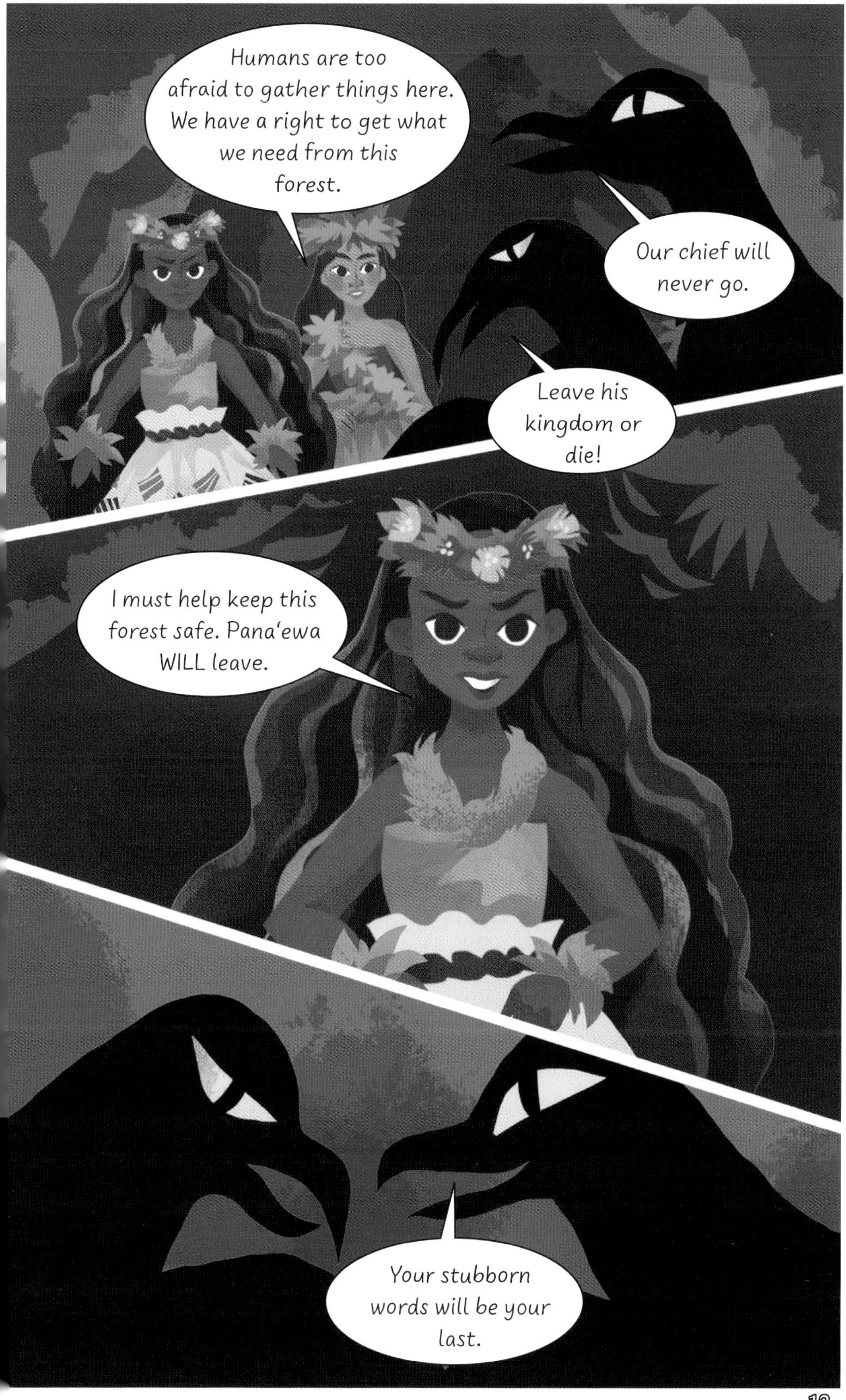
Humans are too afraid to gather things here. We have a right to get what we need from this forest.
Our chief will never go.
Leave his kingdom or die!
I must help keep this forest safe. Pana'ewa WILL leave.
Your stubborn words will be your last.

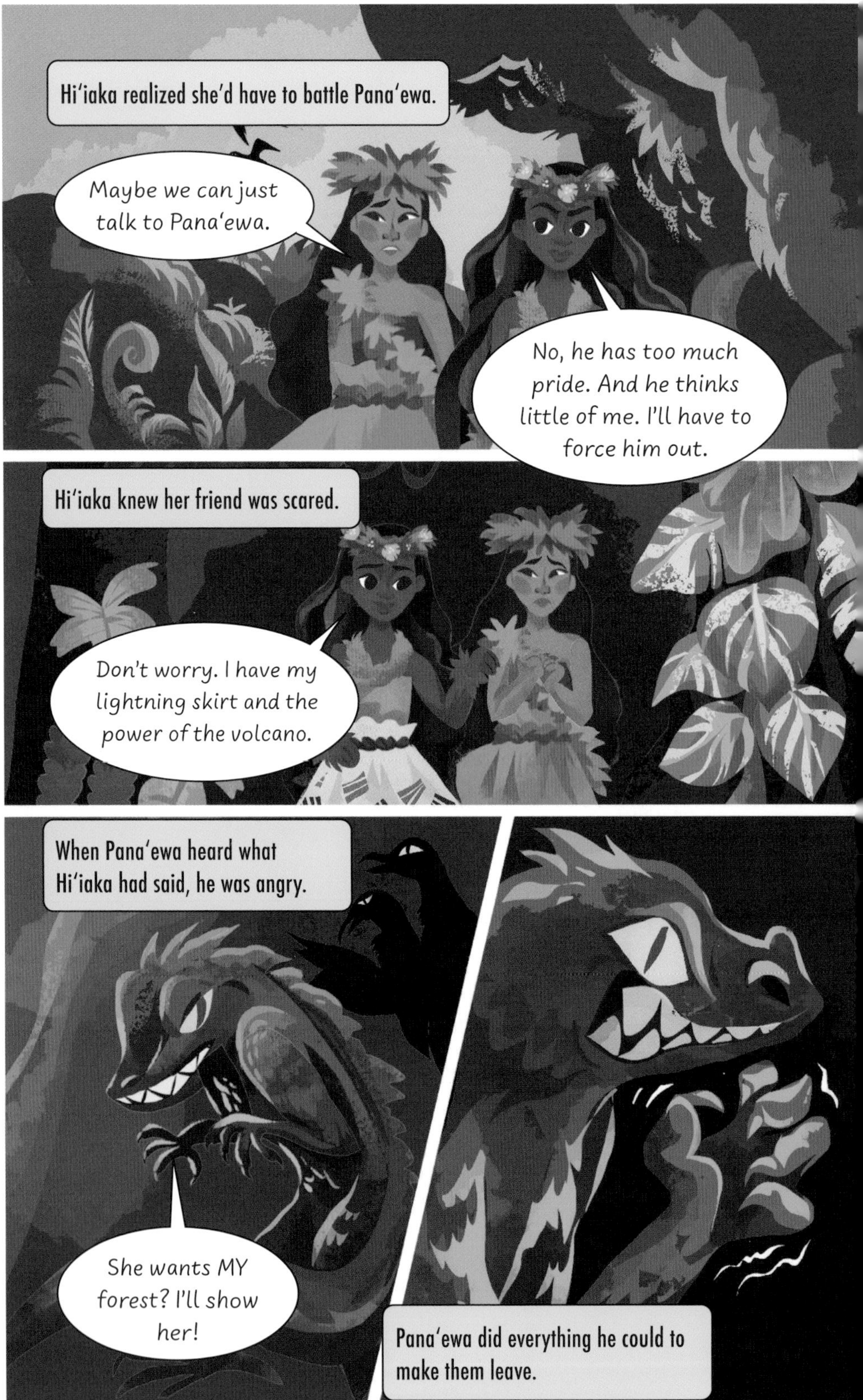
Hi‘iaka realized she’d have to battle Pana‘ewa.
Maybe we can just talk to Pana‘ewa.
No, he has too much pride. And he thinks little of me. I’ll have to force him out.
Hi‘iaka knew her friend was scared.
Don’t worry. I have my lightning skirt and the power of the volcano.
When Pana‘ewa heard what Hi‘iaka had said, he was angry.
She wants MY forest? I’ll show her!
Pana‘ewa did everything he could to make them leave.

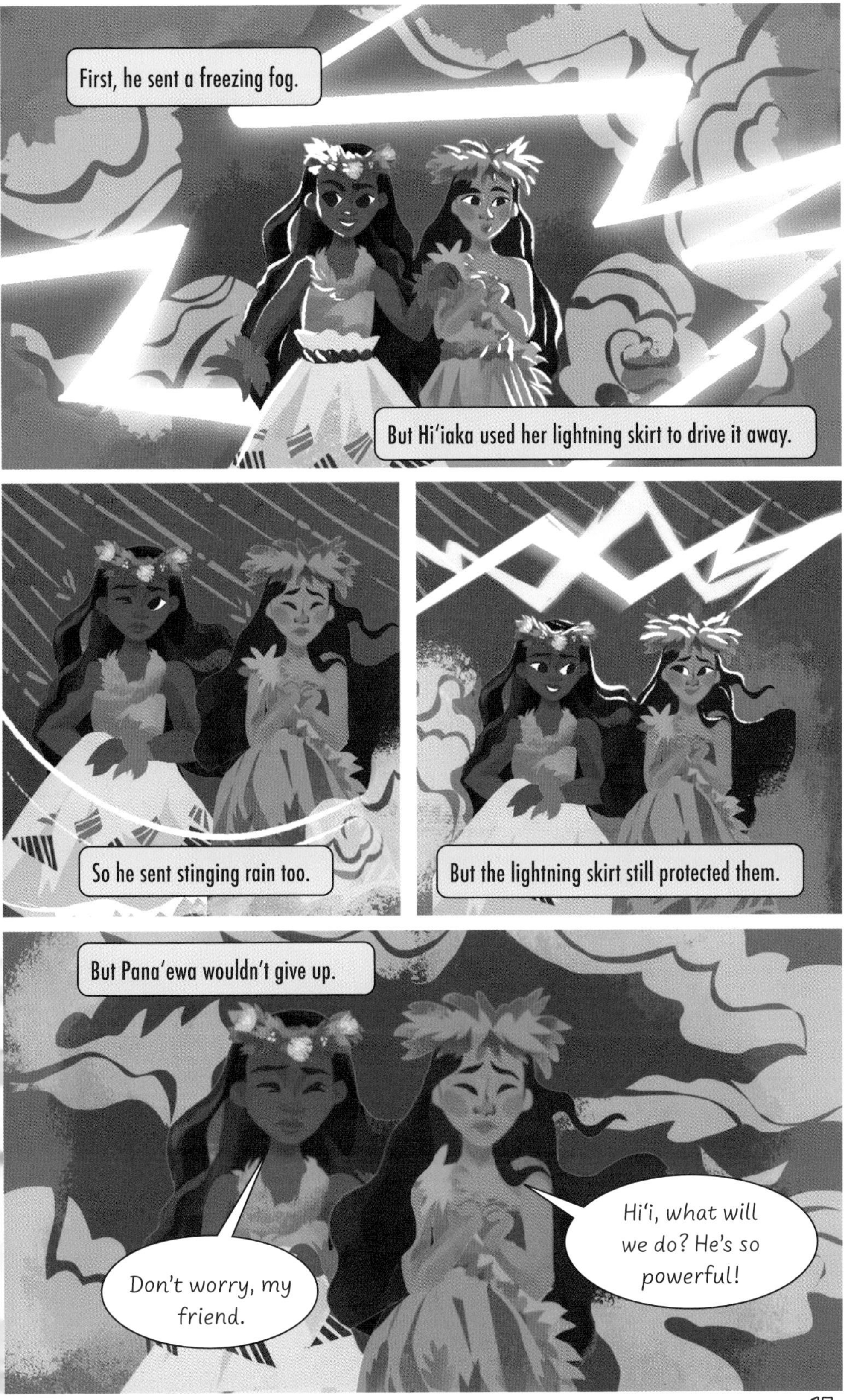
First, he sent a freezing fog.
But Hi‘iaka used her lightning skirt to drive it away.
So he sent stinging rain too.
But the lightning skirt still protected them.
But Pana‘ewa wouldn’t give up.
Hi‘i, what will we do? He’s so powerful!
Don’t worry, my friend.

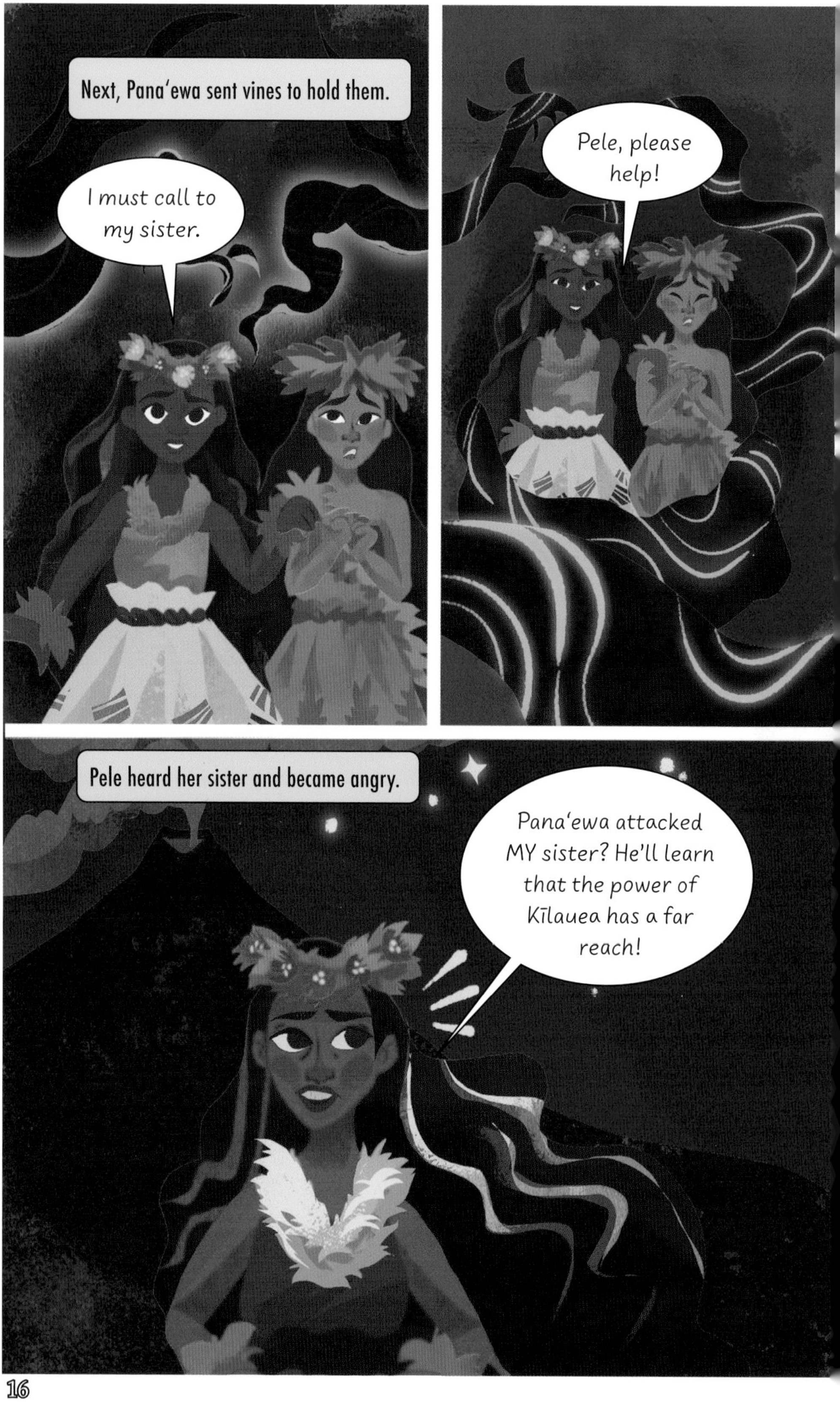
Next, Pana'ewa sent vines to hold them.
I must call to my sister.
Pele, please help!
Pele heard her sister and became angry.
Pana'ewa attacked MY sister? He'll learn that the power of Kīlauea has a far reach!

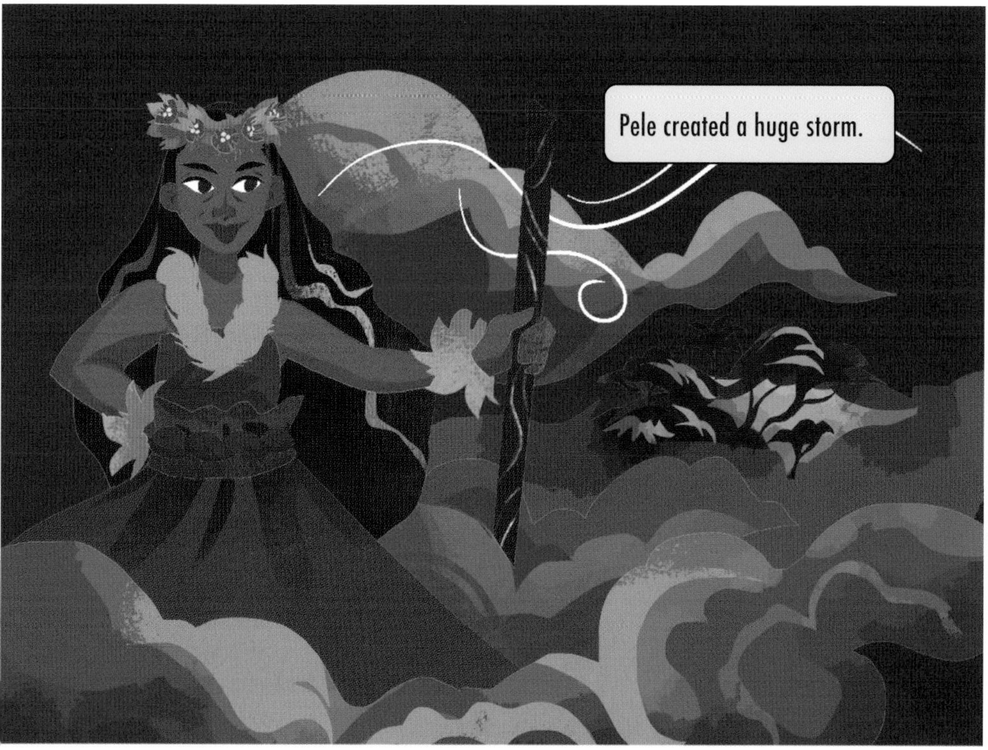
Pele created a huge storm.

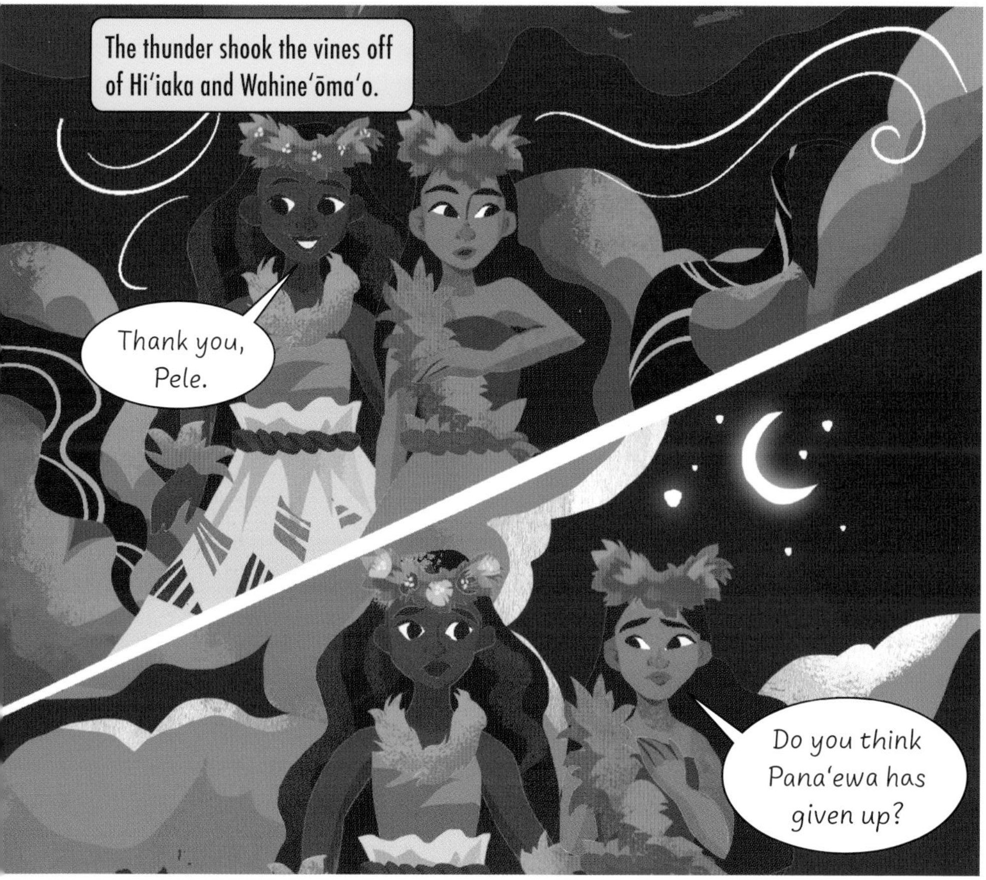
The thunder shook the vines off of Hiʻiaka and Wahineʻōmaʻo.
Thank you, Pele.
Do you think Panaʻewa has given up?

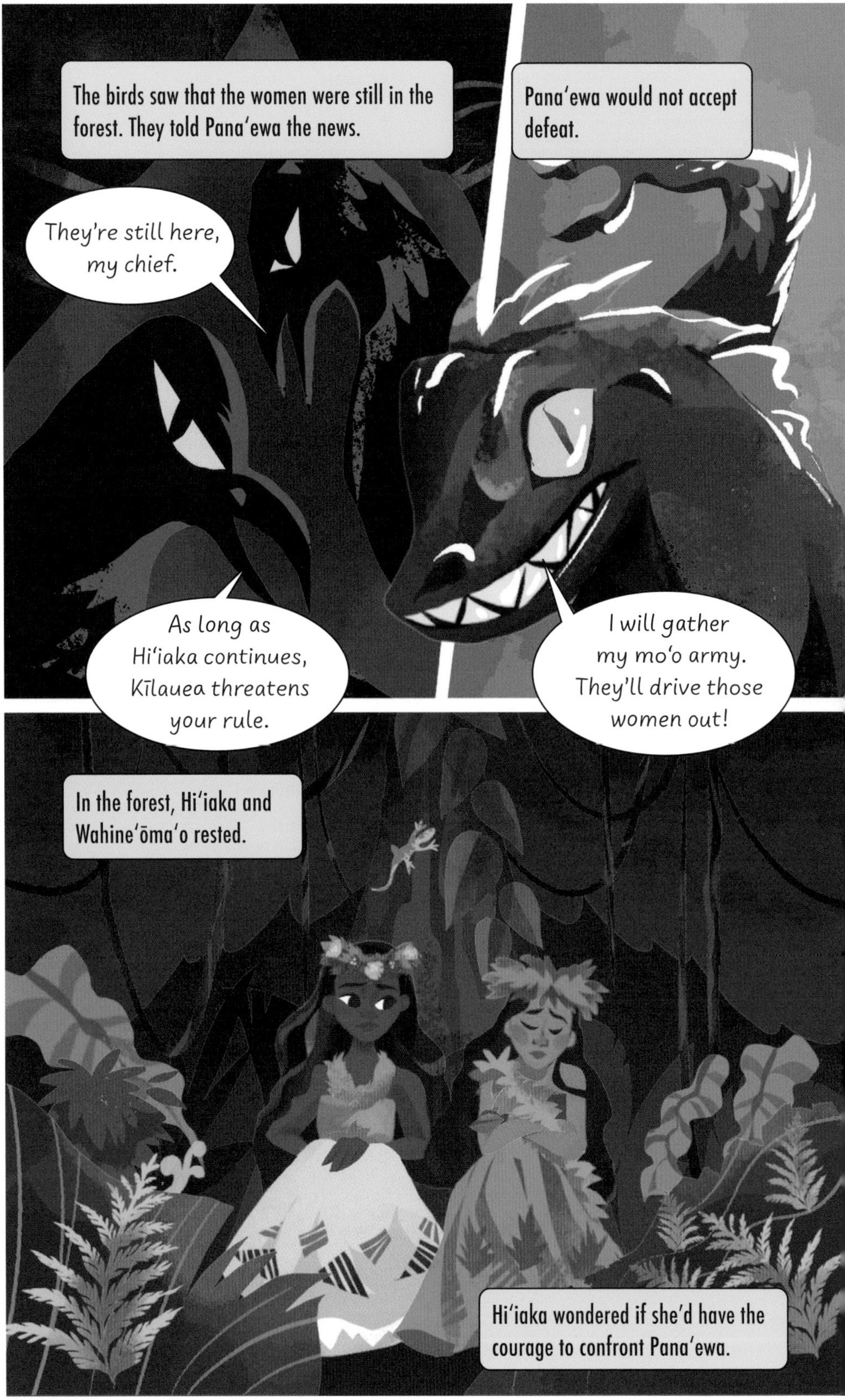

The birds saw that the women were still in the forest. They told Pana'ewa the news.
Pana'ewa would not accept defeat.
They're still here, my chief.
As long as Hi'iaka continues, Kīlauea threatens your rule.
I will gather my mo'o army. They'll drive those women out!
In the forest, Hi'iaka and Wahine'ōma'o rested.
Hi'iaka wondered if she'd have the courage to confront Pana'ewa.

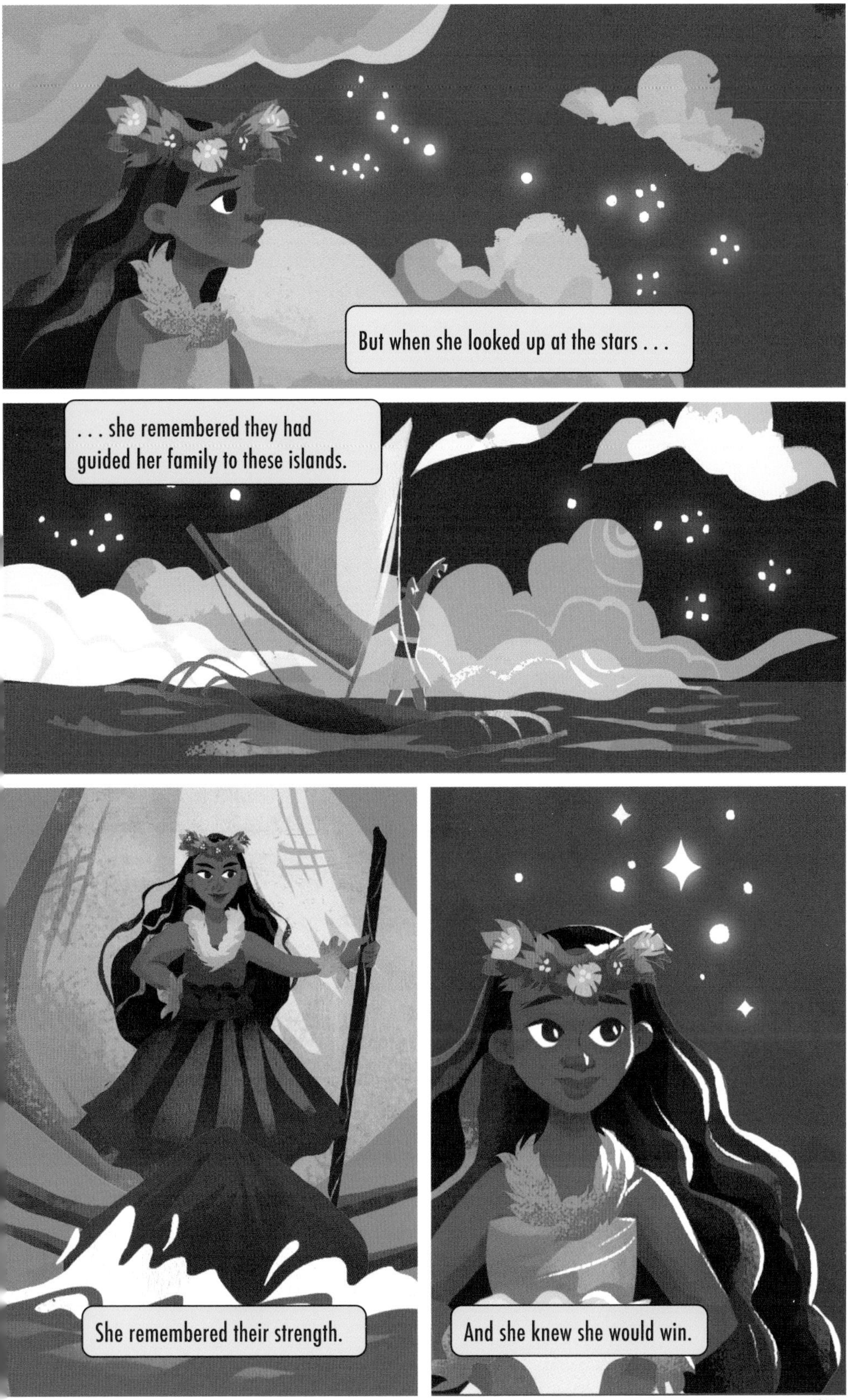
But when she looked up at the stars . . .
. . . she remembered they had guided her family to these islands.
She remembered their strength.
And she knew she would win.

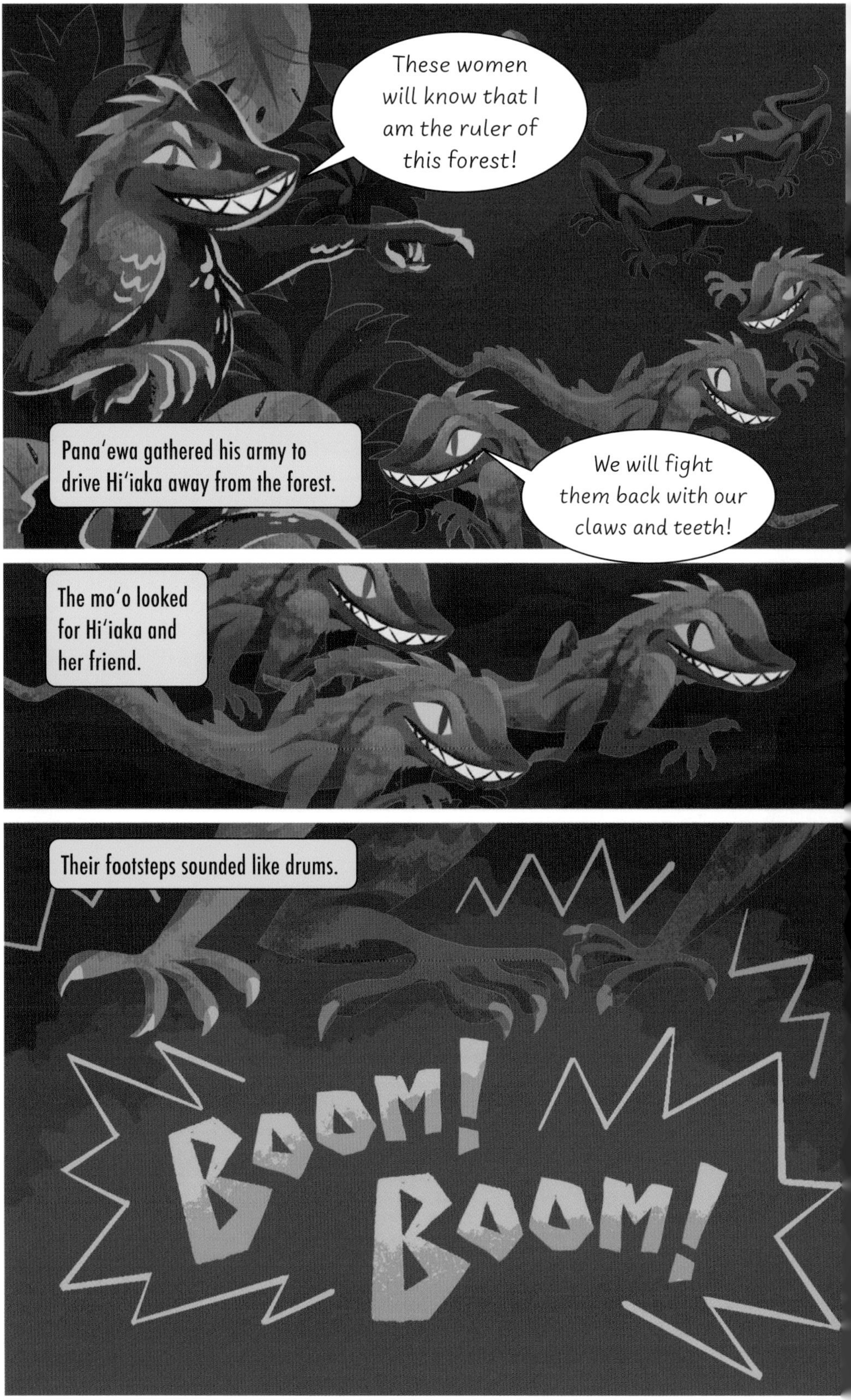
These women will know that I am the ruler of this forest!
Pana'ewa gathered his army to drive Hi'iaka away from the forest.
We will fight them back with our claws and teeth!
The mo'o looked for Hi'iaka and her friend.
Their footsteps sounded like drums.
BOOM! BOOM!

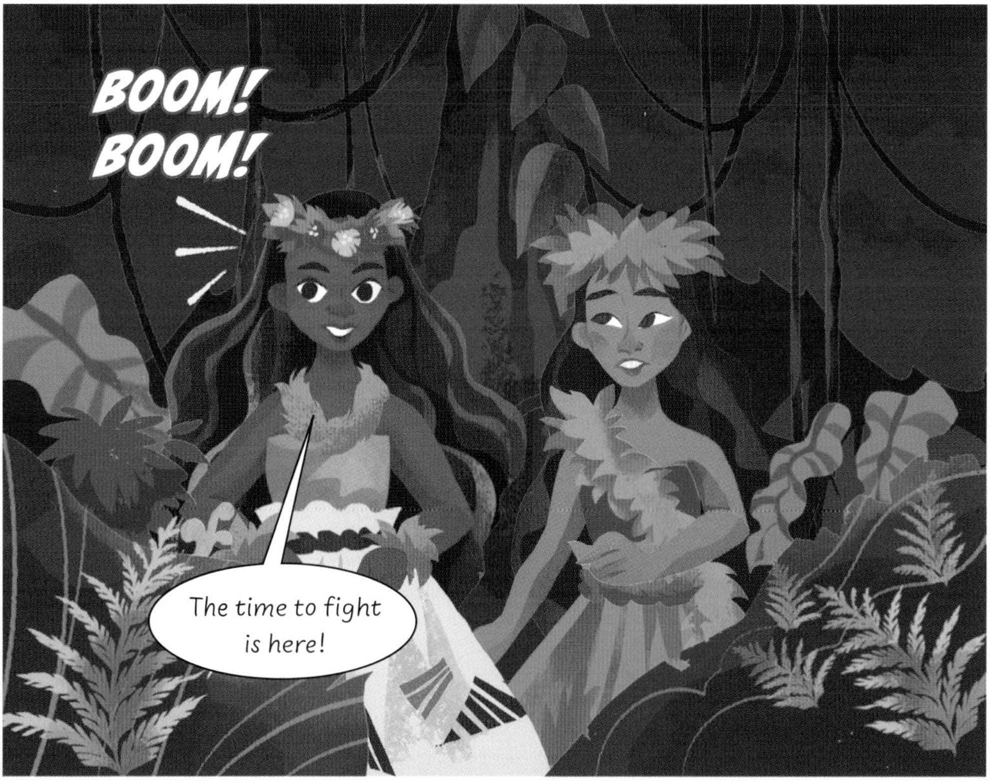
BOOM!
BOOM!
The time to fight is here!

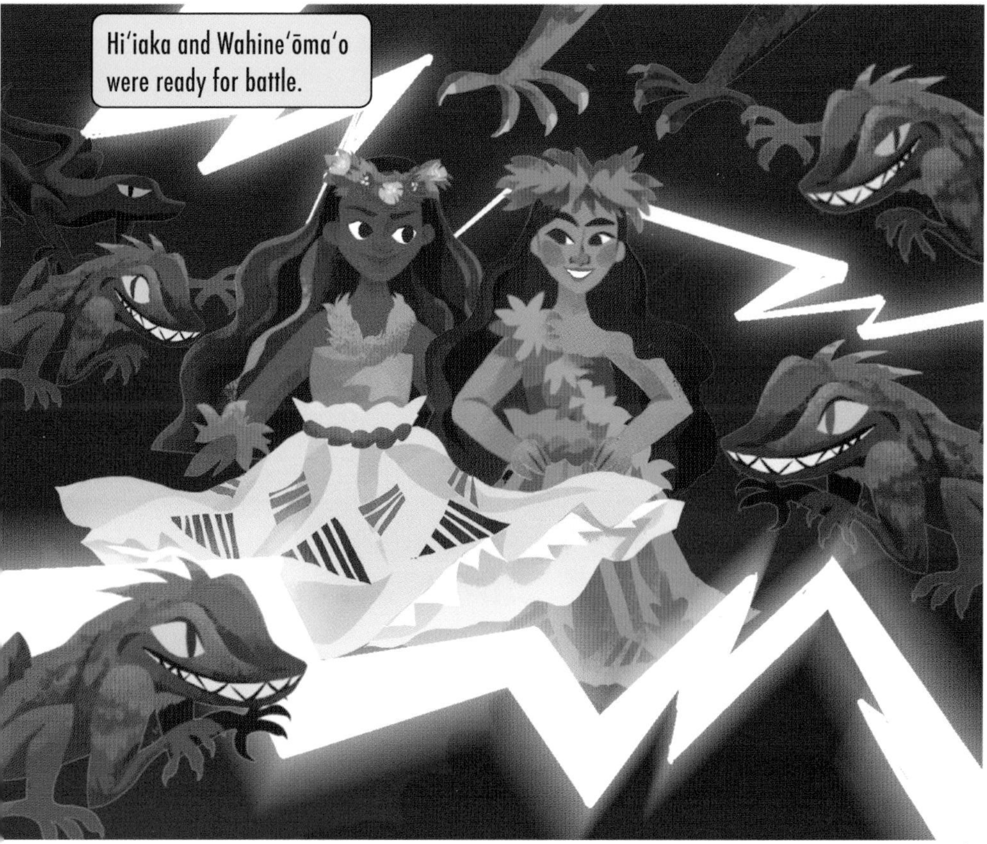
Hiʻiaka and Wahineʻōmaʻo were ready for battle.

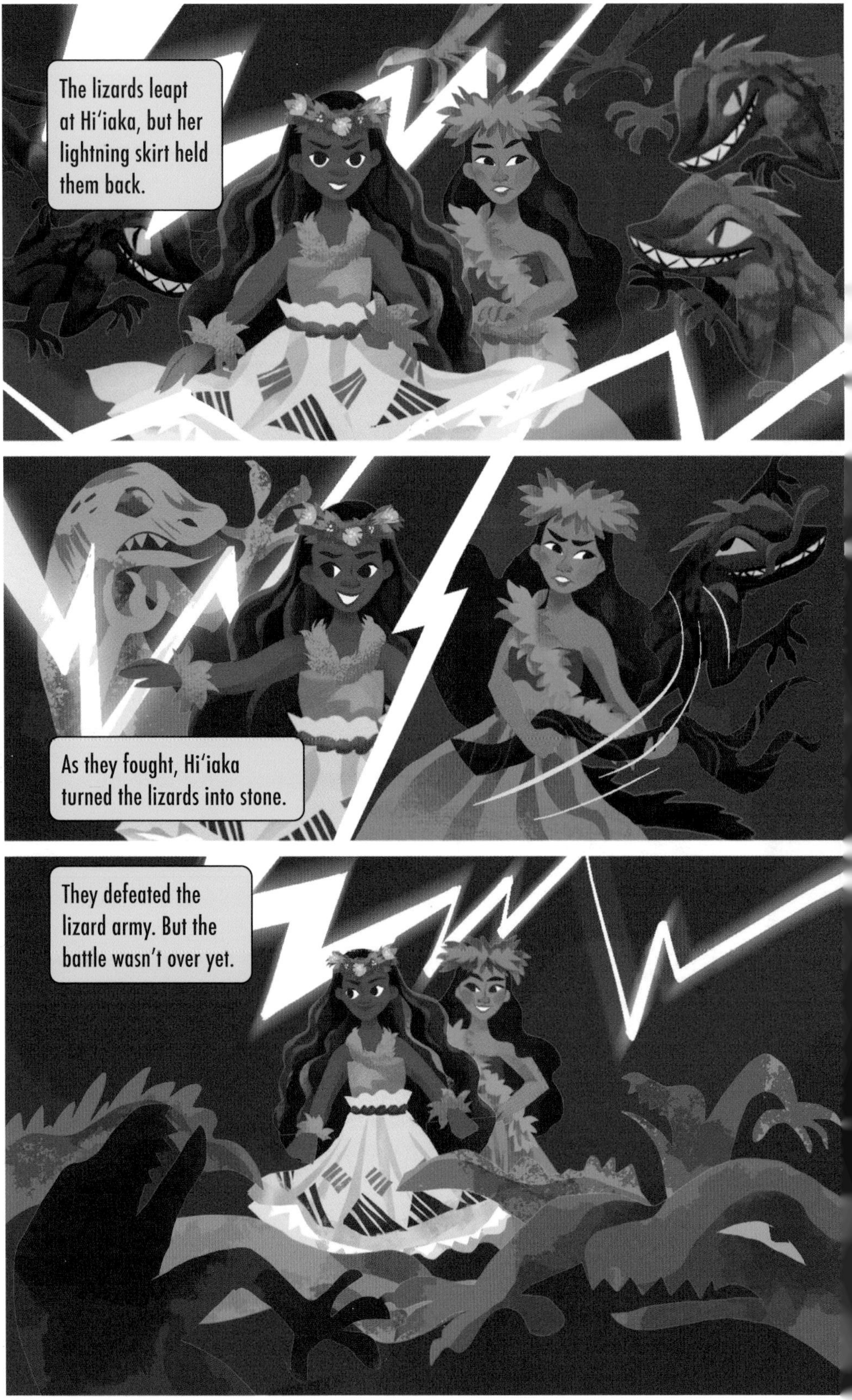
The lizards leapt at Hi'iaka, but her lightning skirt held them back.
As they fought, Hi'iaka turned the lizards into stone.
They defeated the lizard army. But the battle wasn't over yet.

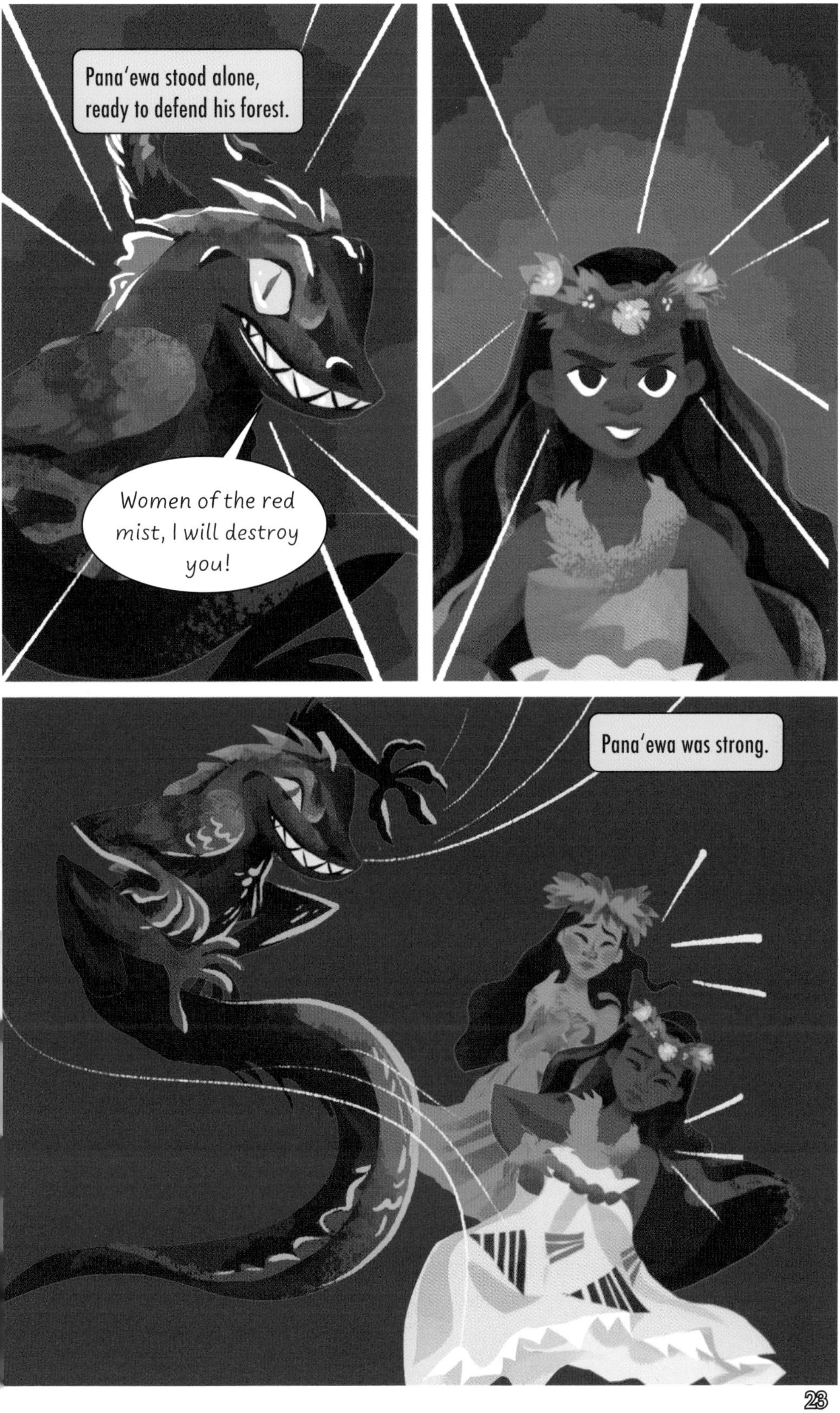
Pana'ewa stood alone, ready to defend his forest.
Women of the red mist, I will destroy you!
Pana'ewa was strong.

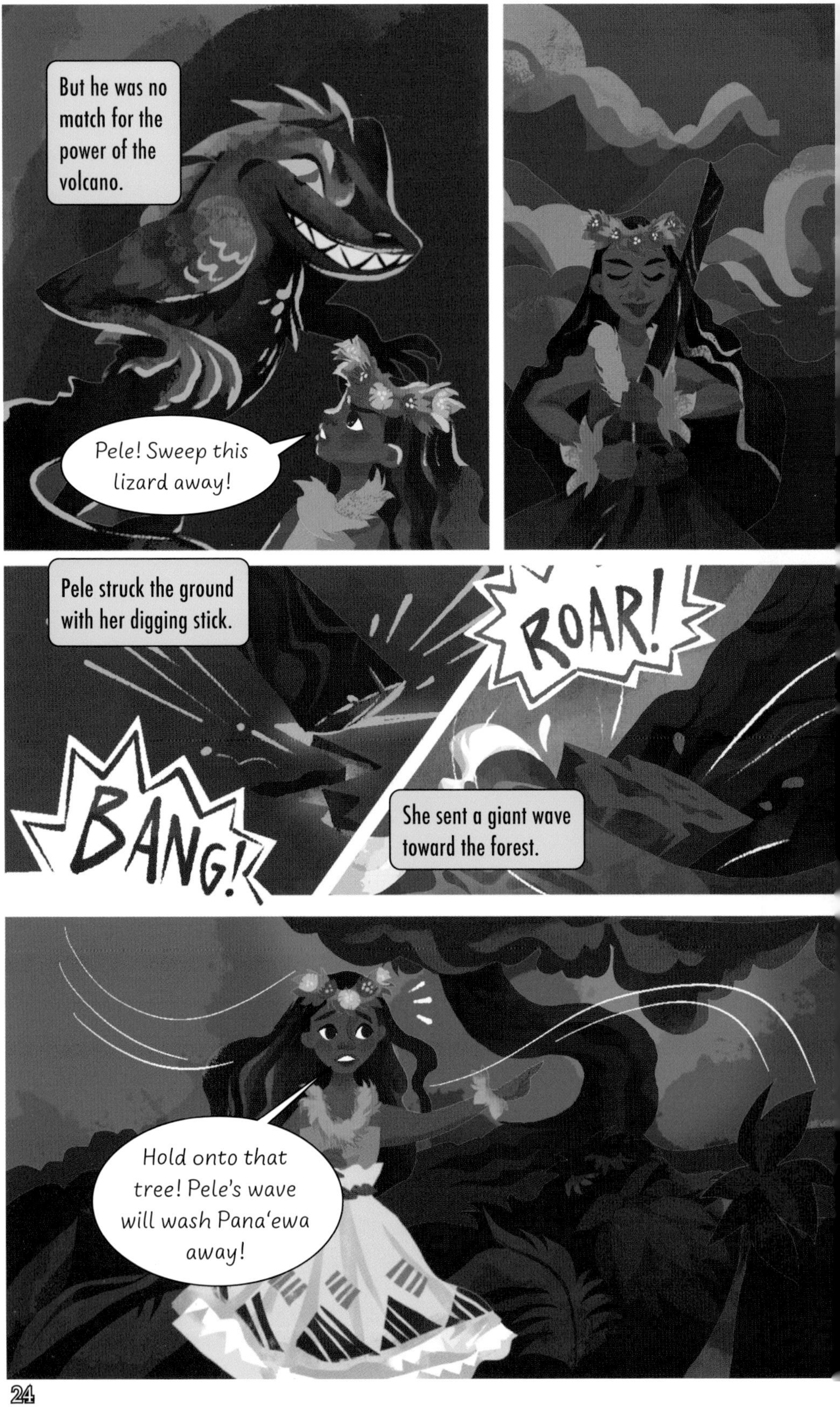

But he was no match for the power of the volcano.
Pele! Sweep this lizard away!
Pele struck the ground with her digging stick.
ROAR!
BANG!
She sent a giant wave toward the forest.
Hold onto that tree! Pele's wave will wash Pana'ewa away!

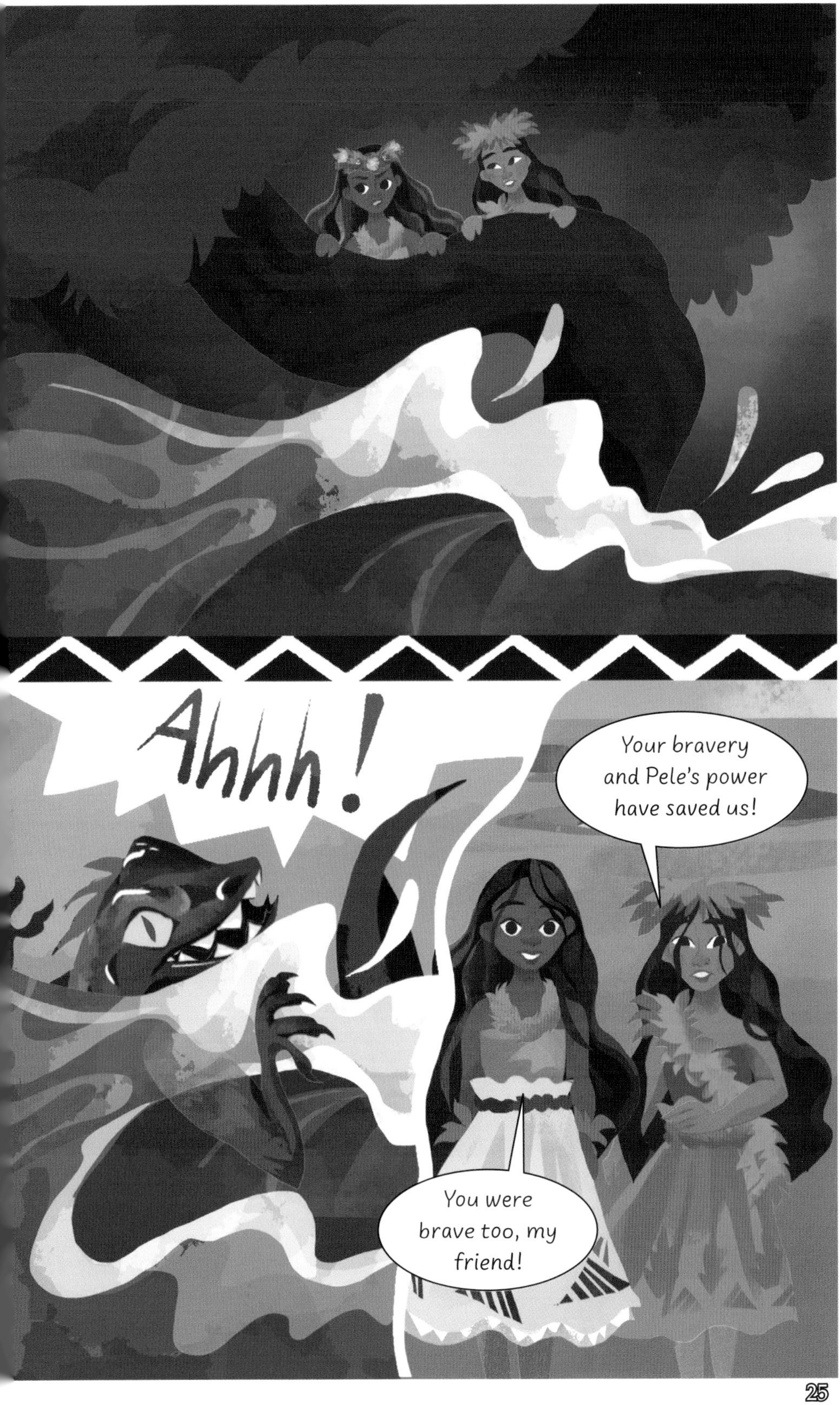
Ahhh!
Your bravery and Pele's power have saved us!
You were brave too, my friend!

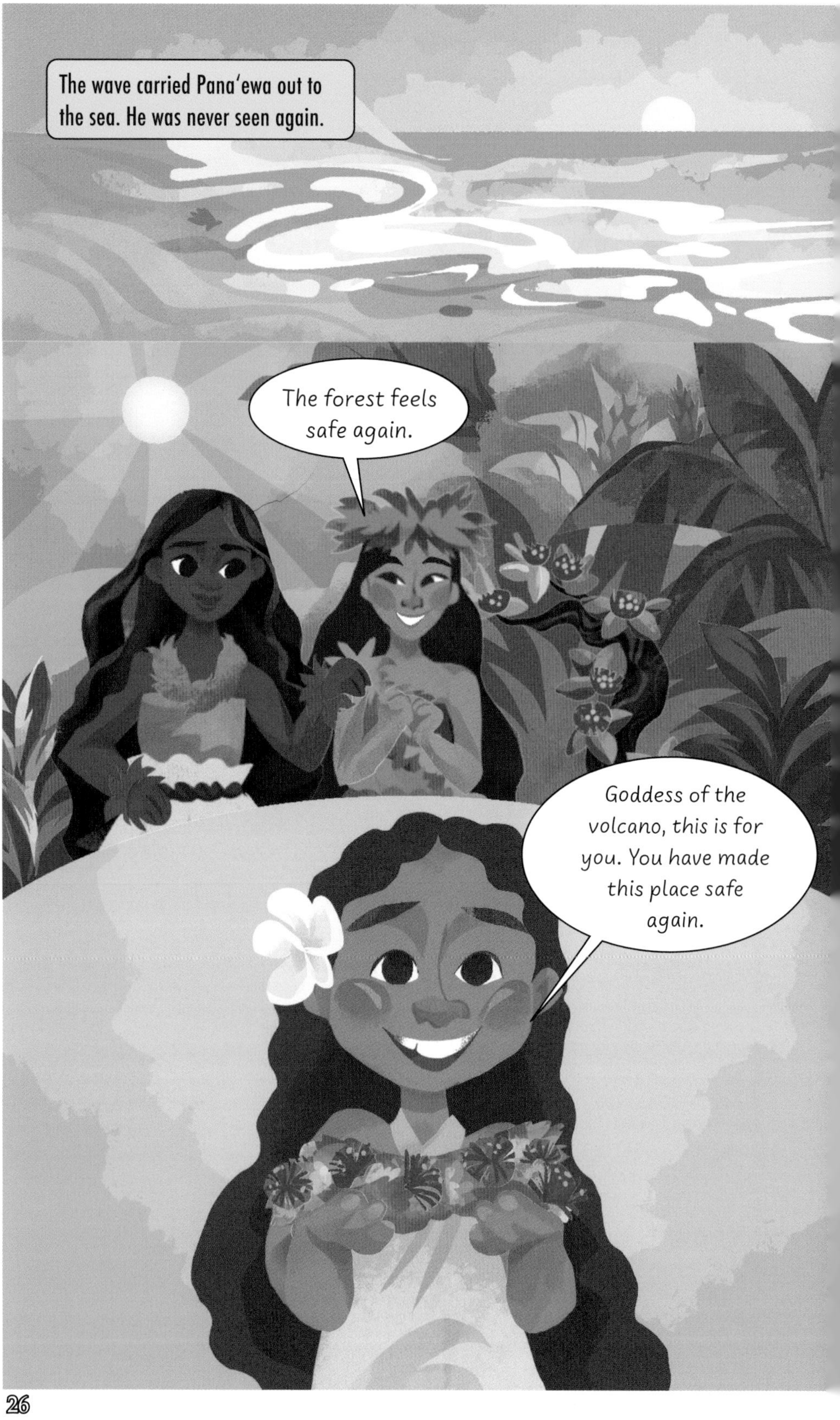
The wave carried Pana'ewa out to the sea. He was never seen again.
The forest feels safe again.
Goddess of the volcano, this is for you. You have made this place safe again.

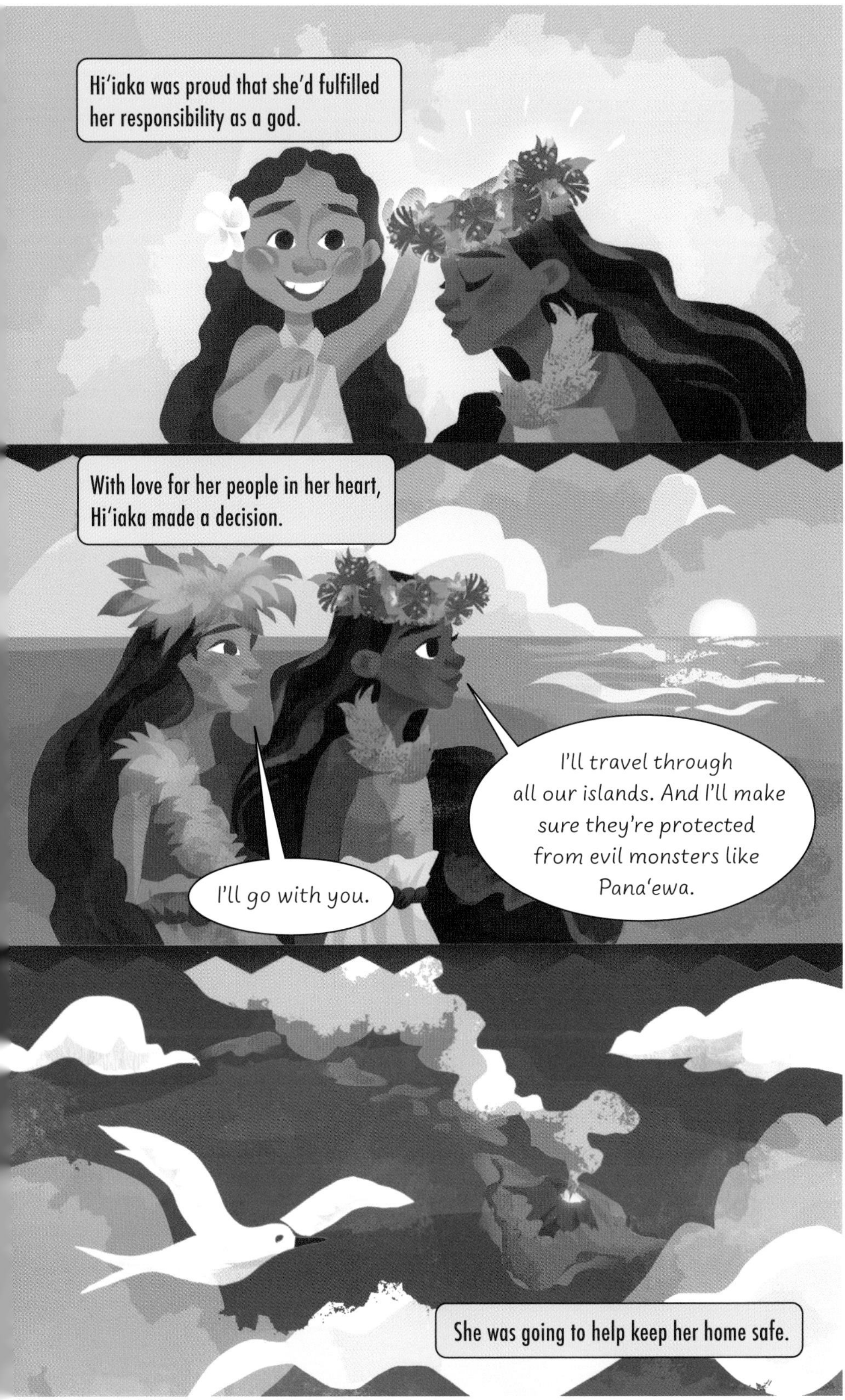
Hi'iaka was proud that she'd fulfilled her responsibility as a god.
With love for her people in her heart, Hi'iaka made a decision.
I'll go with you.
I'll travel through all our islands. And I'll make sure they're protected from evil monsters like Pana'ewa.
She was going to help keep her home safe.

WRITING PROMPTS

1. Hiʻiaka makes the brave decision to go to the forest and make Panaʻewa leave. Write about a time when you've had to be brave and do something hard.

2. Panaʻewa uses fog and rain to try to stop Hiʻiaka and Wahineʻōmaʻo as they make their way through the forest. What are some other things he might have done to try to stop them? Make a list.

3. At the end of the story, Hiʻiaka and Wahineʻōmaʻo decide to travel to the other islands and make sure they're safe. Write a brief story that shows their battle with another evil lizard on a different island.

DISCUSSION QUESTIONS

1. Hiʻiaka calls on her sister Pele for help when she's battling Panaʻewa. Who are some people you ask for help? What sort of things do they help you with?

2. Pele gives Hiʻiaka a lightning skirt to help protect her. If you had something with special powers, what would it be? What special powers would it have?

3. Panaʻewa wants Hiʻiaka and Wahineʻōmaʻo to leave his forest. Why do you think he doesn't want them there?

GLOSSARY

confront (kuhn-FRUHNT)—to come face-to-face with someone, especially in some conflict

defeat (di-FEET)—to beat someone in a competition or battle

lehua (ley-HOO-uh)—a flower that grows in Hawaii

mo'o (MOH-oh)—a lizard

pā'ū (pah-OO)—a skirt

rage (RAYGE)—strong anger

sacred (SAY-krid)—deserving great respect

stubborn (STUHB-ern)—not willing to give in or change

ABOUT THE AUTHOR

Gabrielle Ahuliʻi is a Kanaka Maoli (Native Hawaiian) author and librarian from Honolulu, Hawaiʻi, on the island of Oʻahu. She is the author of the Hawaiian Legends for Little Ones series (BeachHouse Publishing) and has written about and presented on the link between Indigenous storytelling and building literacy.

ABOUT THE ILLUSTRATOR

Sarah Demonteverde is a Filipino American illustrator and designer based in the greater Los Angeles area. Combining her love for the vividness of life and unique narratives, she enjoys illustrating nature, culture, fantasy, history, and other enjoyable subject matter—especially when it comes to creating artwork that children and adults alike can enjoy. It is her passion to create impactful stories and products—be it through design for content, children's books, stationery, or other products. When she's not drawing, she enjoys gardening, playing Hawaiian slack-key guitar, dancing hula, and finding all the local eats Los Angeles has to offer.

READ ALL THE
AMAZING
DISCOVER GRAPHICS BOOKS!